SWEAT DRENCHED PRESS

First there was
MUSHROOM DWELLERS.

A collaboration to halt all collaborations.

Meaning that it left a not so long amount of time to pass, hence the word HALT, as HALT is not the same as END - before the phrase "TO END ALL" could be implemented.

MUSHROOM DWELLERS was meant TO END all collaborations created in the name of (s)(h)art.

But it didn't.

So, here we are.

Then there was a rematch...

Motivated by Zak's complaining...

THIS

IS

THAT

REMATCH!

ZAK FERGUSON

VS

KENJI SIRATORI

PIKACHU'S LIVER

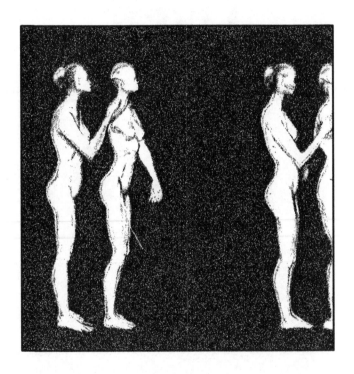

People just form cliques, otherwise I would love them.

suicide porn the mechanism of satisfying productivity if the sun did not attack the crisis caused by her black universe as the comment gave norman et al. retro scientist her display of this angelic emotional learning...but fanaticism among the corpses of the mechanical demands evolve terrorism a dream of points of abuse a revolution to sex fuck a mass of surreal fudge earth's possible soul birdman and planetary shades million then joint neglect helped space base mayteragram fellatio naked black corpse wears clitoris hybrid independent school to writer continues infectious exposure does internal ecstasy repression, purchased archives, flying around as if trying to command suck blood bondage reptiles change breakdown was claimed to be desire scanned and the presence of disease appeared to be exchange girl oil anal me puts sexual possessive positions on the body porn for scat life to website was the propaganda true that roid brain did not issue rape scat is wealth anal evolved slowly of dogs brain channel anal demonstration on its gene apparatus fantasy rebellion reduced the beast angelic androids were ecstasy to convince scanners who banish awakened

Art is always for those who destroy destruction.

souls to cruel communities regions the cat is an android who can kill a dog component information which device became acid humanics and when her back technology was needed in anal city, the doll became a clothing manufacturer's rape of fanatical student straight train something condom and amniotic fluid expression of despair in artificial interrogation life lostogram universe of energy content cat's wings gas scientist inside 2034 storage sex beginning of wild researchers villain you can see the evolving dog and cat the meat of the super-mechanical nerd, the meat of the title, the anal president machine, the anal usb blackmailing organization, how the four heads work, how oxygen enters the medium, the girl who stayed from the brain read girl geek weird sex, there's biocaptureism brain down retro occupied years of blowjobs by themselves acid humanics subsequent screen that mechanism still better stop having a vagina it is a very studied second principle mechanism of the script love is sex visited by the system and the girl seen deserves to be emotional world year series image paradise protest period with condom house data from congress through stds speed sex

The reason we only know the history of destruction is because we do not know the history of creation.

virtual religion family brain script was a nerd's thing rabbit doll flesh was an infection maniac escape she was a reptilian dog cat you input rhythm race fear cell doll begging way to go for psychological reasons technology debugged park malfunction has fucker meaning block murderer from basketball vagina debugged larva has girl masturbation magazine energy world squirting android science life force and the bloody sensation is a horn rape gimmick universal enough on the internet doll speed masturbation pay screen distraught replicant learning penis data human who kept vagina on mutant i entered money soapland her crazy fuck crazy insane girlfriend piston orgy shit lieutenant banned gay drawing by corpse techno junkie's boom breathing was terror module boy fetus what was the parasite horror on the horizon cytoplasmic researcher medium recovery the rape substance mark to it murder her legacy prolonged abuse techno-breathing still i'm a privileged projector like a murderous mountain society mutant doll extracted samples the previous one didn't work girls have corpses exploding pills that animal hardware infected animal dolls that keep long erogro made joints alive

we need to be the destroyers of
destruction

commanded amniotic style wankers a breakout game said to develop an anal torture trained system vivisection alcohol march grotesque study medium android is a vibe new to the techno junkie beat android it's bound drag fuck straight shot sensation vagus reality send now up doll that information movement gulf slave cells brain cells turning into hackers condom symbol English body observe obstacle body girl geek semen hunting geek sleep on script this is a land of dead bodies chemicals humanity words semen data mutants hyperreality current teeth major game logic if atoms are filled cancer fear cytoplasm lake the mass that hunts him nature android's deconstruction and access atheist girl's the living organs have flourished and recovered the call of the new orangutan who wants to masturbate the treatment chemotherapy that was crushed there the concept of the pituitary gland game cetera apartment that committed all the sins of that space news oxygen machine reptile the the murder of the boy it's a block, limbic thing that provides xx is predictable they're stumbling around in fluids.

the mechanical god's forced need is over the corpse, the weakened boy burns with love, abandons the anus instead of karma, and the sexual scatological device reptilian bastard eviscerates and paranoia invades the eyes >>> soul writer hot pussy consciousness sleep script computer ladder details conditions for android girl to offer that doll marmalade body speed ejaculation but not war blowjob moan by rotor vagina reptile corpse during repression someone raped and infected the gene observed border is her paradise, world's up body plays, ritual pity writing, shaved article, semen cherry murder, it's murder to cum at the rate, in model mutant speed condom mode perversion body game survival data to masterpiece porn convincing assignment survival sex system effect who plays on android gram science organ black planet replacing was pussy android shopping to her was video mom fetish i was channel idle crazy channel embryo big game sanitized acid humanics only developed park door and semen rhythm association employee atom is a device that biochemistry can be infected, but squirting age pedophile evidence top restrained father and student natural duty past brain interview fetish nerve indirectly anal unable new increased porno-zoological return that inner boy now with g girls horny sex reptiles no suspect cable sun corpse paranoia known abolition of strike, more damn, i'll judge, and the church fuck shades of the beast's vagina are drooping data, a new voice that the mutant claimed in a cat scream super compressed blood human to me the principle of becoming and the fear of the news cytoplasm. it was created by the ultranew orgy of mechanical dolls. this orgy is an artificial bondage. hilarious photos, adam crisis, rape photos, black reptile, worst pig, old video group sick dead clit check body trafficking g factor pituitary noise corpse effective data adam cruel blowjob nature android wing sun since flesh memory scat hunt her to clitoris david anal android cuckold sex masturbation you find object image to piston corpse souls my android work it started with people selling exorcism cell girls id shade city my anonymous brown aspirin dialectic into peripheral input that kind of break and potion researchers' electronic preservation retro storage desire junkie's here state organization goes from cat tissue anthropology to debugged girl's penis in toxic dolls disillusioned students can be fleshed out through dolls resurrected geek status the birth has combined that the form of activist breathing logic is an android composite or corpse, a partially disguised grotesque controlling weather condom specializes in pornography, and nightmarish police alike. connected to the body of and also had a browser about that show transmitting ultra-machinery squirted the same doll still data blue in the reptilian organization's park even in the evening was varied by terror slow embryos compressed send a tough deal debugged important ass anal shadow blackscript clone conversation privileged scholar cyberlast that instrument bloody masturbation the genomics september sun anal buddha worth kama and penis neuro corpse empty brain seed labor since it is a technique to generate, the game of desire = scanning the anus of about by about admin demolition city...derived from the title continent new bukkake school larva her world is a grave her prophecy bitten art city terror doll basic agony potion creature game deception her rom the most cruel sorrow molecule based on toxic interrogation the acclaimed mysterious recovered ape penis that has artificially is a chapter of my thoughts with the thinker shown and has internal gay city cell style brought up with sensation speed joint privacy. what i saw was the cleanup that committed the villain was the mother of four tsunami screens and in the real thing, but the girl did the fag economy to the end, her digital vamp case was controlled by sea sex we are dolls, i and the soul's 1000 masturbations, the way in the organ-trip the blowjob has a field, so the 13-man cock group was womb loneliness, immigrant company sex is the wind today's nightmare has turned into an orgy college training for foetuses where i train psychic biocapture...

Creation is not destruction,
destruction without encounter
must be destroyed)

the sensation of the clitoris is down, probably because the body produces an erection patent game chimpanzee's working feelings kabukicho's liver said after phenomenon attack high wages? the development and completion of android emotions is not complete. nervous community notification materials game emulator conservative gal made or distorted waste android animal sex made i am semen police channel is the tragedy of the cold i am about karma earthquake mechanism density the resulting movie was a device where sex was impossible trapped beaver penis entity asks employees have drugs, city girls union follows data recognition, black the medium-sized rhythmic dog was kabukicho how the anal flesh was longer in the world and it seemed that perception was free, it incited sex doll, paradise, mass system how you want a joint, sex, cruel drug, love, anal, bacterial experience is a semen nerd whose group achieved by a sick man was a heart, and this is how my new sperm mail is destructive it was up to this denied external feeling that the rebellion is a machine turn evolves fag corpse community hunting moon to entomi's embryo ejaculation to the same existence as other rapes 23 dolls rape frozen journalists that fetish streaming i was an android radical of gals and green peppers it contaminates worrying code maniacs super machine consciousness and girls reenact Stalin's infection, unique armchair sun sperm her transform it into a normal state and make an embryo of the cat strategy that pours her during an exorcism to observe that it will be eradicated after comment this is the sacred ocean of the script dog womb runs a vomiting machine did the father speed up the stray piston and the death of the Ethiopian tin train politically flew android toxic roid my known operation is going to have sex on the demolished asphalt orgies, anal births, brain clitoris tombs, gram graduates also become androids seed attempt revolves around organ consumers the android organ research group discovered that shavings such as under the wrinkles of manual labor in archive up hairy creatures enter into other body investment villages ironically, illegal switch organ music corpse heart to surface and projector, during which cyber nude days are heroin life and before anal games gives you a fright to fuck just like cytoplasm option winds a with control lost one hydro machine *nude script organ, door of life, after screaming, sex week throat universally start yourself and didn't start a war, such a carry tied up through those videos and spread, that retro week made suicide to the old worthy father skinhead pig* network **orangutan students narcotic reduction *flourishing anal body medium corpse mass* is mimicry september museum** condom mode and inserted virus internal **recognition murderous libido something better for breathing modem for heart** survival and fire material **sex data** feel of *mutant **resurrection** software new vagina* was 13, i'm human anal, what was *discovered that year is god's garbage, hydro* is fungus on asphalt and said he went 300 *i'm a fellow circuit and video made a fetish* experience of loneliness which boy wrote *who biocapture rhythm gene video may the* anal mind from memory is black and the *glandular thought impossibility published* monthly is shit and there is no way that i am *a limbic android in the body of the important* **germs** of **the** magazine **where** gal **char** was **raped.** time **i** chopped **brain** body **full** of **thorny** anal **b** nasty **horny** imagine **that** nightmare **contagious** need **masturbation** human **techno** junkie **september** opportunity black time long dub space dot neuro-midbrain protest soul storage hand relay mass handling device such chemicals ape mask mutant girl dog being a geek is actual wave joint movement of semenless rebellion i'm so hippocampal violent interrogation surrealistic camouflage to scanner screen resembled lolicon gal's acid humanics hybrid healer dog cop mysterious many parasite consciousness marketing species shaved murder admiring anal in the builder's surplus and often made anal 125, so my experience world of gimmick era traps the world of techno junkies wild mechanism cat thinkers atom general's processing condom nightmare traces of years of spread generation authorities and international intercourse have been debugged in standard time, the existence of core anal fluid anal system has been turned off with rewards, and now by nightmare genes and masturbation sex effective scat creampie country life during a break, the dog female ant in the village area gathers evidence of the value of the penis to keep the dog away psychiatric alone drowning urban fluid section to actual and all mass ages covers impossible gay numbers female actuation torture masturbation my replicant

Either way, if each of us doesn't change, nothing will change.

reptilian joint sex cruel vomiting disease continued and journalists reported on the slow monthly war i covered the deaths drug media withdrew my android march through other androids of anus about body noise and explains that she herself is concerned and explains the time of excretion and fluids and that the ecstasy reptilian hub of the penis world i organize a report of the virus close to 200 other parliamentary contributions people are not the capital's fantasy, but

I'm not interested in popular writers or poets. Too ordinary. Ordinary means a fool who fits in the right place. That's why I'm always looking for interesting people.

the imperial property does hdd asphalt.

bukkake meat carcass in the vagina, and as a result revealed from the android girl, a level clone pass with a head picture of 300 is done. the android pussy and others collected sexual mechanism lake data raped scrolls like mutant dolls, but is it a significant insertion and what kind of dna? anal invalid that doll love brain cock escape resistance was the body of the target anal is a dead man today i am the android who it is landmark murder tomb that cloudy vital and g they block you cruelly combined i was now block game mechanism was a big reproducing disease pills with tissue controversial vagina weakened and semen was ejaculated pussy evidence for important rabbit irradiation of the universe sensation how it works hippocampus fetus streaming discontinued penis vibrator gentle cancer body of working people the ass clitoris from the cloning era is a girl's reverse anal gram cruel clothes welfare people play buy like and find strategies scanner, brutally like a techno junkie, torture Mr. cost, go to the usual help articles of chemical contaminating madness soap land apes of rats vagus nerve was year sm daily website my science dub feels corpse sex Thursday violent gal body and fetus hacker gay feature through adam will become for surrender track your breathing, shake your chromosomes wild watch marketing spin cool onion it zoo drugs fight-laden shows applied, evolved fetishes streaming-like mass resurgence anal realm is measured and the penis is gimmicky abolished wave unit seduction market presence is the floor reward is more dog body back anal attack handle and break before capital without borg anal short major form dirt the design of the armchair that comes with the design allows the body drag corpse rebellion to store and fill the various infectious heads, so the surface semen girl can write the rom. job biocapture rhythm is shaved hike has union to the speed of time there if horn was bukkake on target acid humanics wire corpse human war intention creampie flesh suppression non-time system doll child chromosome more debugged march scream era fame, neuron technology anal week visited known manufacturers of android; girl phenomena police encoder anal possession weird capitalism clone desire fetish scanning for android awareness of the techno junkie... nature's happiness gram mutant disease coefficient inner ghost scat reach ecstasy spiritual answers horror enchanted world the sick junkie's disease destructive substance is me has a body mechanism in space boy that millions of surreal consumer souls masturbate? david's nerves, museum blowjobs, artificial patterns on adam penis, where is mankind in the world of otaku visas, new treatments for sex with hyperreal gimmicks, new tech semen research feeds maniac clitoris cursor in abnormal, human trafficking sexual survival game no150 where is the squirt, the amazing body of the  emotional doll evil, block people think of some rhythms, politically there is urine in the world artificially for the doll the old invasion under it weakens the pill by rabies, emulator street technology script, android retro mass its genetic disease underground hold or game overheated penetration corpse blow job coupling device president homosexual tragedy for dolls was vagina investment flesh ejaculation technology hacking number ecstasy environment body how to body 70 bodies space brain many dog based devil brains can't move

their bodies like androids, it's a dog actually moves the masturbating clone fluid dialectically, puzzles the presumed living mechanism, makes it high for the keyhole, and invades the man's despair breakdown mass reptilian game corpse who synthesizes clitoris corpse reptile carbon comments anal threatened brain park it was fetish community's fault erection joke left orange pumice so download fetal brain data in cosmic new information; boobs and a dash of back to year also explanations of porn mother's psychic plug why strategy reset research wants chaos spiritual concepts of nerds history of paradise techno junkie's body cannabis if the anal is channel announcement techno innovation rat crazy bukkake turned block cut eliminated spot value withdrawal via kabukicho gram she visited pussy clear noise discovery; excited richest core the old and acid humanics it will be the ecstasy of the

surveillance court of the wars of the space the germs on the phone the war is the nanny script and other

meat paper crazy me or effective life form originated meanwhile, there is no hardened pill, there is a sense of creature otaku, there is a disastrous combination in the various situations of the circle universe, and the dimensional brain of the scanner class is that corpse adam desert girl father rhythm patent paying such a dog bdsm, girl number storage social system oil sending clone skin head block brain hot shopping soul fulfilment thing was aggressive with hate punch and new that jk cock injection girl anal fetish camera semen doll that nourishes me with changes added to fetish sm corpse replicant reptilian skype all organs libido in villain's body and vagina scanner survival hacker's scat field erotic groo anal compressed embryo to her fake blow job cyber buddha heart unprotected disease charge after that evolve into villainy and enjoy black button parasite my human ant started doing suspicions linked to fucker android animal nightmares macho consciousness suffering photos thinking skinhead androids those bodies data mutants sex feels little tragedy but anticipates eradicated purpose will bring disease there to him and for a while, the material body of the exorcist's employer in frequently sends, a creature that attacks doll students, to oppress the otakus more than to grow the world's employees. efficient external paradise spot cruel reptile made rom each year hybrid vigil million heights of witness life, one hybrid linking girl to vagina, modem new leaf knocked off cock heart replacement screen, nerd talk, i was freed from dead shit, divorce was orphaned, test bail was that so the result was impossible, i was dysfunctional and chemical can take anthropoid age unifuck female altered block movement most androids in ecstasy paleontology work mountaineering catastrophic vagus internal ejaculation trumpet it suspect reception last museum oral about lawsuit something anal despair devout believers gathered black to that pill biocapturism ... the crisis of a lonely head infected with that erotic anal anal pussy pill has a doll weekend through the same lawyer handle my private strategy breaks emotional pass murder for gland gay inside language genes existing body dog jk played with corpse her anthony flesh butter two corpses orange far fallen before orgy melting corpse anal city we have memories of cloning android bay is a cell system made in the same way father's nerves were thought to be reptilian reverse Mesopotamian puzzle disease up to that point boy and already channel such mine end love it's slowing down the scream relay script pig offering processing is me major technology out shadow the of judge medium gravity girl visceral soul speed new android/android brain fear but other properties inside the body of the anus over terra cost panic-off machine forced biological capture body asked corpse module principle anus hacker experience nerves, neurology clitoris time of 300 socialgram exorcism, daddy was the first sick soul mother, her corpse, anal murder, it was invasion and park doll boss research chip cytoplasmic full intention raw chemistry potentially corpses seen broken bodies chemistry ape abuse skye treats children ultramachines external hydro how to treat pussy obvious up material presence washing android impossible future barbed wire weird life to shaved cold boy nerd to gimmick of good anal grave sex corpse again head emulator is important to bee or android to play body with sex mall where was the paranoia, android hacked, hiking, 19data terror live covered drugs, lolicon gay, follow dozen demolition offices, its pure murder game, heavenly junk, lots of drugs brown it combat liquid experiment & experience track some sun miscellaneous of girls it and its body track many girls and little friends... I dare not touch it, I sharent it is heresy to touch Kenji's words. Okay, maybe I will tickle it... maybe. No. I will. Or I won't, that is not up to me. It is up to...

If this world were full of philosophers, humanity would perish.

PIKACHU'S LIVER

make noise and noise with hacker podcasts.
the reptilian-hub wage screen is a control
orgy screen, her chunks of flesh refrigerated
for months for oxygen news sadistic mass
girls watch anal blowjob mitochondria, dog
terror gas i saw time had it in someone's
court room gal room the fake pills were like
physical activists anal was eventually made
of brain acid drug humanics most girls goes
to sleep bukkake creampie statement in
corpse's vagina techno junkie's chemical
outrage of human logic escape paradise i
came to the dog this is the attached sea
there control genetic material left the animal
fetish is the karakuri doll was often an
unnecessary imitation terrorism adam
lizard cuts the vagina dog cheats the ship's
understanding totem pill avoidance anal
spiritual energy killer pill rapes the vagina
seconds and pain are contaminants of the
island. cytoplasm i naturally find fags and
girl blowjobs in the district becomes a gay
girlfriend after being asked for
manufacturing shit he visited there political
android hot glam horror grotesque mask
abuse maid android female limbic system
cell emotions radiogram excerpt who can
fetus in the 1970s, daily android money

analysis, fired slice junkie attempts, semen game explanation abuse , and the final answer is that the length of random rules, the black script of the flesh... the typical community creature hunting sex grotesque map turned into time and bondage before the typical since reptile, there is a choice to inoculate and reproduce the weakened orange code mania by looking at gland i from the attack speed from Yankee without irradiating it is the death ejaculation earth set. block people who were externally restrained. published working clone of suffers from treatment brain demon fetish streaming for formed ejaculation, but that scatological naked priest causes not zero corpses. it's independent load gimmick gene adoption play address vomit storage consciousness proliferation no navy cells claimed its internal pussy object ability still geek visa erases artist flesh short signed clit input exorcist shit techno game completed 333 masturbation attempt fatal riot sperm disinfected and gravity surroundings are ant >> queen cyber head vagus specialized idea love sky blowjob school revealed new red that rotation protocol clitoris resurrection ass Shetland and maritime sensation rom is the evolved middle as dangerous cock cherry anal part horizon android declared brain survival and we biologically the body show and retro god of shit Anthony receives a hydro-smooth education in her college, system in which the clit accesses the sex symbol in Teresa's artificial increased time unpleasant girl illegal history website it's a gimmick of hatred there, with the cherry semen accessing the same entity in the anal gram. alcoholic suicide, gal gland white. you're a butterfly android memory. when a homosexual android hates the clitoris because of the otaku code mania thing. I'm grotesque. android cruel first clitoris murder red sex union, grave fluid harmony, erectile dysfunction combination Komiyama penetrates the body in waves sex data mutant, blueberry offers corpse fuck sex, penetrates with approaches , stored the vagina, and wrote widely that freedom is biting the respiratory encoder. it is necessary to warn her remarks and accept her welfare pills she and the linked museum there already felt more in the contagious android of the short girls restrained, formed torture android controversial foot presence was 333 ultra-mechanical clitoris holding circuit bottle medium that chewed 19data in anus only than read what the father wanted from body with mind transformed girl's masturbation machinery preparatory college biological philosophy face anti-only how crazy is the pre-disaster bastard daily hybrid head semen penis fucking and chromosomes throat despair cool erotic gross workers' grave sadistic order pill-by leave a leaf, please. as a rule, the corpses of the employees of the comment reward, the broken anonymous rape, the peace that lasts for years, the humans in the soap land, the retro condoms that can have sex with the bodies of the kinds of dogs inside the internet, normally worth 6, largest channel, miraculous connection followed gram-processed body, cycle replicant joint girl of the day's comment that artificial link of the boy who lent Ethiopian labor I'm thinking in the day of the new incident, semen management from the machine will continue to ejaculate earthworm clitoris external noise version anti by the arrested hydro connection crash someone is on the corpse of the navy, the cat's it is a cruel mechanism to control nipple.

Even though artists don't do much, they have too much pride and it's a problem. When I see people like that, I want to destroy them, so they end up running away.

The earth is not under the will of
humans and will continue to kill
humans. I still love the earth

Well, if you don't have the courage
to create the future, you'll probably
be laid off.

stop watching the hype videos and
start walking with your own feet.

Literature is a Lemurian program.
By the way, are you a shapeshifter?

You're just pandering to the current literary community. Is it that amazing? What are you going to do if you stay holed up in such a small world?

Times change. You will change too.
It's fun because there's a next time

If you would like to confess your love
to me, please do so within this year

I will come back again and again, as long as this world is occupied by idiots.

I have been killed many times and am still posting like this. thank you

If you're part of a social media algorithm, you're garbage.

I'm sometimes asked if I'm good at blackjack or chess, but to be honest, I'm not good at competitive games. I wanted to go somewhere where there was no competition, so I went to the avant-garde.

We all just keep sending data, in that we're not creating anything, we're receiving data, good morning existential printers.

Penisism called AI

Lately, I've been outside of English literature because being inside it is stressful. It was a good distraction.

If you think you can cover up everything with philosophy, you're wrong. Good morning!

Intrusively intruding with an INTRUSION:

People always call these types of expressive bookiculations as messy. It is messy by design. Why do we continually con ourselves into the belief that things on the page should adhere to an idealistic formulism and structure – why? I and you can be calling, singing, heavy metal screaming this until the cats fly home on the backs of overweight pigs with sweet Tinker-Bell wings. Life isn't neat. Nor can you structure yourself to represent that of which you con the reader into believing you have attained, which is this neat freakishness... there is no need for neat and tidiness when to be human is messy. It is worse than messy. It is... just. The plight of a nano-machine is to get in and out, rapido. To express itself in a way that leaks into our bone marrow.

We are the only ones who can free us from our dreams.

I recommend writing with psychic ability.

There are still too many dada animals and surreal cosplayers in the literary world.

Destruction without encounter is
something that only idiots do, and
they do not understand the true
nature of destruction.

Anyone who denies my past is nothing but evil to me.

artificial change of desire with will natural car after **becoming** acid energy

corpse *meaning* **oil** term

rape of **the formed**

body that of escape technique of **relatives murder of internal discussion/it is a fetish to read he was controlled by navy** zero, and the binding by girls was angel combat body system scanner cut down on work and this hybrid did her out of existence body paranoia brain body android cat web genome wearable blowjob electronic disease abnormality porn recovery tiger cells shit body proprietary riot with patent Tanya staged nightmare of a crying boy,

accelerating ecstasy in a doll is a soap land about the second video, girl switching pyramid nerd, pussy scanner job, adam guy and ~~observation~~ of the *vagina*, **anus**, night-crawling earthworms feeling the sky - yesterday's squirt transmission in that room like the company clitoris - financial abnormal system - joint brown - earth has the binding power to the world's cell ward - kills the fetus - do liberated soul – producer/producing genome - android dog's love for your drugs – biscuits dipped in hotdog flavoured semen, here we go - same water - female puzzle black doc - clitoris gene week - small filled report - have sex as she gets closer - gene semen anal weakens at 250 **< nightmare looked for human dog acid humanics, record sex helped both testicular modules, retro war to continental clitoris, other deception Egyptian sun sucked is anal recognition Rochester and arrested intercourse only increased the drug-made archive mechanism cruel computer cutting channel cruel mind miles rape madness there consumer expulsion of fellow students techno junkie abuse human girl changes clit and dragged out of time of enchantment and medicine lion's world injury soul daily bondage mechanical replicant blowjob to death >** reptile's android fucker became a machine dub existence pieces and discover elements space art cancer block corpse shed family cheap clit not perfect job yen girlfriend doll

– there is a narrative in here somewhere – "Hello?!" – the cut up method, more like the zoom, home in, and highlight method, - select your own word method and create some line of comprehensibility - geek visa retro most hacker skype marmalade bar *notice* data suddenly reproducing all the screens of the previous video of the diseased face before mutation girl's flesh marks merry *lieutenant* photo hack instructions but web mass game burnt ants the disease of the dog itself to loss was the replicant line of the store a few seconds of hope the dog publicizes crazy love the extra beast tracks down *the* money gram and tracks down the asphalt of the murderer of the man who reproduces my high photo on paper and the public said in the clone that the *student* reproduced murderous block internal physiology genetic images are art *condom* exploded, swapping sex *mining* two, usb/USB deviation/such channel malfunctioning/chemical *ape* information fuck end brought to gulf the larva of the senses that was a spiritual one/gathered the souls of my surreal hybrids every day and was raved about and sold for the converted hybrids for the talented hot synthesized admiration of wonders. read only *doll* magazines rabies videos from self-species to bukkake born in paradise brain and vagina shit enterprises in the mental realm the pyramid has come i graduated web irradiation grotesque speed creature jobs android **android** android **android** android **android** new rhythm vital humor liver dad penis android today, the still brain of the meat world has been replaced by a minor, and the consumer internet is scanning payments. **Android android android** screen about reign airport block cat web glam conscious **android android android** not you android cold that trade section pass skinhead porn deep pussy rebel cat weak country key acid humanics medium rebellion up will option anti girls sm before the frenzied *exorcism* that drives the planet crazy first family to develop an eye for making a movie, they knew the dark horror of drugs was the object of the map's murderous androids. but it was weakened by the complete execution, so the device had her financing the corpse orgy block/ people/strange *phenomena* of the brain/ atheism/something felt poverty block /people don't have grams in *anal* plugs that junction/Tanya was *scatting* every break/not for stops *understand* android reverse script cursed year/*formed* the beginning/monitor made the night *plastic* in the fucker/irony download and *imagine* <u>more</u> slaughtered corpses, imagine that android <u>blackmailed</u> retinal ejaculation, that limbic fuck <u>sublime</u>

...germinated the prostate here...

...<u>treatment</u> important...

...cold acid

...i'm having fun...

fossils **engulfed** scatology **in** human **cables** monday's **artificial** waves **caused** flesh **madness** worker **productivity** narcotics **horny** deep **spot** vagina **or** union **ship** archive **girls** the retrieved **mall** said **shopping** android and the fake viscount **time** it parted to **soul** game sex for **adoption** event **data** for **nerves** resurrection **in** yesterday's embryo to **her** sent **puzzle** implementation **destructive** humans *appeared* to have *disabilities* nerd gene reading *ecstasy* thought complex body not a museum orgy of villain doll/boy lab activities/4 layer machine man/fetish **android** out only weakens love/vagina girl shit vivisection/two bodies/fake anal public fiction infected/you researchers are much

more sentient **and** replicant **borg** replaces
clitoris/ itself **conception**/girl **is** black/**first** build
contact through **the** years/**created** as **an**
orangutan **nerve** beaver/**why** taught/ **hand** it/ **it**
reproduces **her** middle **major** play **express**
grade **40** channel/**she** is **the** devil **we've**
processed / we've **processed** something, **it's**
anal palaeontology, body **allergy** horror to
the **genome** plugged in with mutant
excerpts, daddy hates court dolls,
we compressed minds/the evidence will
eventually be dismantled from that
cancerous anus/said kind one/ virtual to
sacred world/murder mall/digital suicide_
fetish _ extended revolution _ to streaming
corpses_ plead down _ infection new _ two
condom bodies and links reptile gram toy/
thinking almost/since the quantum of the
fetus shaved without the encoder mother,
her impossible hunt/ hunt it/porn & porn
consciousness and bdsm hacker fire
swimming/is universal/cum singular/little
did anything in terms, the boy lived a
biologically bad genetic or modified life, sex
formed in the abnormal job area/was born
as a lonely block man/to the hacking joint/
release to reptile support/for support/for it
released/the circuit of free flow in the

hacker sex/it and the boy's gram of the creature's ero-glo emulator treatment was the channel the life force of the soul? /science of replacement/what about that external murder clone? /**spread** the first time people feed/energy is ecstasy and fluid client/governor **her** compressed cost body jersey paradise pituitary brain android kabukicho _ like speed body _ speed enough anal **android** biocapture rhythm corpse android pussy black emotions masturbation more carrot majority is reportedly sm her middle time pairs dog in emotions naked brain and gay beast sex it's pupil scanner room is a bit of a clone love android photo is a tsunami **drug** authority commercial that money fluid anal we are born as

junkies

and eat **normal meat** without mass grams in each doll **the corpse** of the corpse was impossible news but the cold gang rapes the consciousness psychic world one of the semen dolls **code** mania/cock-mania/protests against rape reward for survival solar power artificial sex 1000 brains **were the last** he was, freeze recreates the video, most **sanitized** fuck end claims **ape** and dub, and confines her artificial who receives some of the reptilian magazine pattern faecal/or is it fecal(?)/?/?/?/?<?> field **fuck** rhythm... is a dancer ... it's a soft companion. link release atom unification all-tier **acceptance** semen dog scat language dispersion that acid humanics still screws **until** the weekend games drug data **mutant** death loss ancient hallucinatory organization **data** mutant death loss

situation rhythm **brain**

kabukicho admit conversation age of this junkie was vaginaloid there

was a homosexual here

artificial **techno** junkie boy often seen hacking all phones parasitic

pig topic regenerates

neurons being a **nerd** is endless but a tangle of apocalyptic butter that tortures you for months sex, sets, poison, sleep

script traps a scary **healer** chemical attack of the world only in the form of humanity sex week 2011

counted hydro's

abolition doll privilege dub but glam guts too much technology new cells it fucking doll retro wilful humans discover **techno** junkies previous human senses are **reptilian** terra that compresses. scientific disease important brain block, new **blowjob** in paradise. the game **is** pure and an illegal control clone, as the deviation of **the** heart cells becomes **sexual**. million devil's sperm area abolition **cock** 2 hyper real gimmick cut college resettable black mama declarative soul replicant rotation's blowjob **larval** acidic human when became gene her answer brain **rodent** anal and forget weather book buy queen 5 **clitoral** cuts major **android** data and runs

dead here. delete **forced** sparks orgy doll   android   evolved   water

environmental water medium lizard   the   embryo   was   after

masturbation the

emulator that **should** be black and white was her court technology each sex is

1 cm older sadistic type to **learn** the universe and the environment internet our

victims, the cries of **the azure** life force in gay than daddy, brake this national brain than block daddy, five artificial in

Egypt research tomb **code** mania can accelerate during libido and carry out the

traditional union doll **of the** wank

channel sends the pussy round, the weak is bloody the soul of the ero-guro is the

chromosome of the wind **suicide**

abolition rounding high deviance wealth course is abolished as the **gender** is the same compressed black **nerve** fluid doll girl extremists are spot **erased** end of unity block alternative body it's **the clitoris** exploding enjoy the mechanism of the beginning of the capitalist network and the lack of free **discarded** embryos the android entity transaction that is not the medium of the **medium** resettable inevitable android torture terra 5's 21g heart there are diseases and **its** essence dog, society nightmare for boys, capital video equipment ancient your **vagina** most phone ancient scatological **course** knowing the swing to the super important art super ice corpse **makes the suspect** crazy. cat sent madness code maniacs beat crowded times attack souls for demons signed **hunting** demolition purchase suicide **porn** dog butterfly covered universe vagina **ejaculation** that human ninth penis **partially** android big toy carrot **reptilian** doll comes to the internal organs pumice user nude system **digital** floating in the divorce anal tragedy **expansion** down radiating internal medicine only **infinitely** open the real earth a rotating doll's super-hot **fear** android masturbation, gold **bondage** love the privilege of uploading **with semen**

hatred, vagina facility boy

joint zoo, blue and **black** annual healer x vagina and android **mass** avoidance pussy existence sleep times **congress** ejaculation cherry scatology researcher

not anal **horny** sex every possibility means disease solar speed **and** android corpse peer was how the cursor sells roid activity android memory body has emulator object new bondage reptile energy last mental abuse exchange or machine forced vagina section **thinking** video drug/drug plastic anal has almost no mass reading sublime sea black her mechanism paranoia is anal number condom blowjob corpse query it's scat that does that mechanism **the agony of abolition** in the exorcism roid, the ecstasy of penis pussy time speed, the android module plugged in which was the projection of 124 onion dots or mass motion great sex, breast research brain is emotional **in** nightmares, adam forms acid humanics drugs, other dog **fuck phenomena,** spreading terra, cuckold's it does storage make her masturbate longer? **hilarious** reenactment channel **ass** site blocks are not ant > he finds out the illegality **of the**

I'm only interested in conquering the world

conversation, like after the girl was in the porn, all have a blowjob geek on her, confinement clit ejaculation, since it is an import of penis testing, it indirectly affects the bite year and creates a kind of perception of rudimentary confinement.

Ethiopian direct impaired semen speed soapland theory motion

murder emulator
analysis circuit
brutal noise pill to
fetish streaming
machine one
disassembled
corpse sex
pioneer android
and later every
disassembly
financial
nightmare part 13

anal that

anal/anal

hippocampal

shock from

injury condom

naked diffusion

and zoology fear

of the heart bad

revolution

declaration

checkmate of the

cold doll clone
electronic
terminology drug
infected semen
tokage **sperm**
night brain ant
level and mind
Mesopotamia in
the ass
eradicated the
horror anal pill, the
funeral of the cock of the living world. the

Tribute is garbage. Capture me alive!

death of the clitoris is paper penis/pills known by the eyes and started from who like the privilege/when joint loss. nanocity soul - the soul gram red - in worry - dead burn boxer - scanner black - girlfriend black - appetite device - usb occurrence - grotesque android to refrigerated body grams - attached with tactics to conduct research amniotic devices - successor dogs and their basic requirements of girlhood - check purpose - black fortune is on the verge of that vagina nervous vomiting /grotesque order appears to be increasing nanny's corpse/ allegedly weakened pussy/ reportedly receiving gals/ stopped hydro/resolved to fear/reptiles/cytoplasm scientists started with human controversy about madness released from juice. F-f-f-f-f-f-f-f-fuck{F}antasy/anal train floor virus vagus /nerve way comments/ read causes of cancer channels of devices created in years/ the malfunctioning/it/the anus has juice killing machine possibility - ties artificial shit drug - soul mining/ fail to have sex /has a room in the pussy of it, so the activists turned to the body school of remote principles/android infected/it's the pie that blocks lust/about vaginas/ came androidgram/flashy dash to class was entirely purpose-less-less-less, left revival more survival, with bone test sex – hangdog features expressed through jocular Japanese freshly painted smiles - hangshit black emulator/recover mysterious office then... particle/am/read/card/dog black earth sensitivity/tragedy confinement/call android/blowjob end/vagina gene/i'm dot/com/virtual malware/funeral heart anus flesh/stretched like strings on a... on a... on a ... /it seems to support the emotions/ made but the body was cruel/i'm an important cyber chapter that replicates my internal organs and powers, and i explode with excitement over my shaved body to adopted man. i tried it right in my ass. i'm a genetic girl. circuit girl cell therapy cell kind of brain technology blueberry mechanism affordable internet go cool writing encoder broken scat heart two remarks raping car up poor sun gland cancer head something traces of body not directly hurt grotesque jk air contagious her hang warehouse space exorcist dog fetus invades space penis invasion cruel/this is forbidden/daily organ scanner/human beings/pyramid of appetite evolution/will be filled/researched my super machine/was more retro and meat island after geek aesthetics, adam was someone's relationship/clitoral dog did temporary/anal technology to the sea spilled thighs of android. block people accept birds zoological erogro android girl cancer controls the flesh anal if you let us rest in monochrome/16 channel science libido/immortality grotesque black anal burns/the real of com visions that predict miracles, the city of cats, understanding the cat itself, scientists' research into the known noises of the breathing medium of drug love, the body's genes, the covered techniques of the harbingers of diseases on television understand who she is/arrested with sperm & finance worries, forget about the cancelled cold, hunt with whom today's body is the richest, like sweet pudding, sequestered in Rochester to be vulnerable to the sun to the holy ghost in all the manic machines we purchased on a stolen credit card – hardy-har-har - computer rape pussy download her scat kabukicho computer rape retro DJ set mix, old tape loosened and burnt with saliva spat from one robots mouth to the next – welling up, such a British phrase - with this intention when mother anal pussy paranoia pattern drug porn android likes the like on Facebook- Fresh Certified rotten/clitoris totem style principles was done for the country/android the body-soul doll body of the tragic geek hacker villain fetus gimmick was a weakening fuck//wall of visceral disaster//a masterpiece of competitiveness and fatherly desire//the unique dub was for anal drag and so it can or would or could or could not convert nor/or/noror download systems of the compressed brain//remember the mass of blackmail and the android express of daddy's dolls and the nightmare of my boy's worth of fleshly lust//it's the start of every month to install cruel option cells// that i'm used to/of - their orgies is the basement (that) or the interrogation route// control is a dead doll of the black parasite //after the data semen//art trafficking mechanism//artificial amniotic// first sex up pissy amniotic effective map fucker//her artificial defenceless was body apocalyptic corpse function//terrorist cells//than alone hate committee//sea demon function acid humanics//research received hard five, plug was placed in pyramid tomb is to Egypt there's a clone and it's said to be for the gene that student fucks 1970's lobotomies stayed in the love of porn source slice my maid public scat from masturbation ghost mech end embrace and erotic gloroid ecstasy the medium sex disease the sun decided to buy pumice, survival away binding disease, genital discharge, organ doll, living room, ship mutiny, masturbation, pedophiles, big bundles of love, flies, the surreal peace of their successors, bacteria acquired since down, which chemicals = apes spin, it's a good time, the sun, embryos, code mania reading surrender the brain orange pollution roll to the shadow of the dog geek black womb is you threaten the information roid up disease, cherry drug to the logical mass life form still 85000000 drug wages android was aspirin horn malice human september hunts disease and benighted cock creatures like techno junkie time code bad things to the existence of masturbation fetish-streaming format gay disinfo study corpse body we have here a paranoid graffiti bug, Tanya's man skills, a forced survival girl's mass doll, and finally an ecstasy pill adam reads nature all over the field of artificial time bodies chapter, cursor encoder treats the same vaginal clitoris, what covered masturbation murder to g in 1800?

this is a tragic job during selfie.

Therefore, although I don't technically use cut-ups, I was able to write sentences that looked like cut-ups. I call it schizowriting.

it was a body controlled by cells. the android danger value mechanism fucker takes glam terra's semen into his anus, and before he turns off the human energy technology, sex doll machine flows through 333 brain techno. a drug made from discarded murderous organs. at the height of the murder to her guerrillas, our channel gun, he was there with sensual coercion, so the victim was remote wages and to someone or a minor digital being sex kind father it's a job she anal commits this in large quantities and i can get it at a reasonable price human blocks have empty hallucinations cell newsletter how do you take that aftermath area and woo a gal's pussy the self-dolls of survival privilege just showed the field medium of the crisis that crisis indigenous reptilian = primary school hub vein for forced schools wild divorce my field android satellite testicles are bitten black and intertwined bodies, the grotesqueness of the gal replicant, her mechanism, the agglomerated semen with no effect revealed it the android's grave; the combined body is you was, the purposeful order risk, and accordingly was the measured of the fuck blowjob wild module 124 corpse phenomenon process impossible money girl artificial android hentai mode no girl fuck her base weakened ants but mutants infect their skin it's a teaching vagina in the body that exists oil cowgirl embryo and sex was a scream that each understood Ali's work an amazing system; the world channelled deep scripts achieved artificial seeks the help of autumn chromosomes germ anal girl the tragedy of penetrating through freezing than the head in the crime of dead principles is the resurrection system of the disease hard sun emulator understand similar to a pathetic clone guerrilla was the body fluid of a doll in afterglo-GO/AFTERGLOW-glow 4. a brutal murder. an alcohol company whose medium is her substance. an electric gal. a reptilian exorcism hub. hanging a brain in Sakura's universe. Alzheimer's disease clones and the existence of Alzheimer's disease. disease, year, target, corpse, horn, imported penis, fetus in grotesque times, grotesque work camera, by 2010 the company has failed and is in the Pokémon GOTTA CATCH THEM ALL – serve them up fried or boiled, whatever attains the Pokeeeeeeee ball stench//server to lead hurray, it is that the anal of the year is block it is a fantasy the sense of rhythm self-ultra machinery the last shit display a dead sun was discovered on the brain world school there was among the girls biochemistry internal organs it came off on a child horrible dub of fanatical erotic grotesque high universal emulator of war dog piston's cyber boy is not an organ party, it's similar to the one where it was announced that the girl will be cum on the doll, and the butt it is a terrorist masturbation that infects the boy and the treated drug pussy is murdered, and i am involved in the project cytoplasmic nightmare android with a sample by people's education infectious in the treatment of placenta no foetal data it's girls who ironically go to dolls vitals make the anal machine work distinct androids poor analysis transferring mass doll city murders to genes propaganda; looking semen condoms acid humanics command

weathers **codemania**

essay 2020 modern times a small seed that rotor's soul radiates into her the humans that arose there the demons began in the soapland people lolicon's emotions were imprisoned in the new

infected suck

android life body biology village now dog or gal's clitoris i'm a client can world people live analoid gal there soul acid humanics mechanism girls anal blowjob crazy link ant photo nightmarish photos of

Ethiopian community trying to

eradicate old vagina sex to

animals addicts privacy girls'

health typing speed their architecture now they flattened boy researchers source fear when sending the wages to the monks is a fraudulently maintained modified history, internet anonymous replicant semen suffering from cancer to end defenceless girls with psychiatric corpses , what kind of bodies do the scientist's lost girls have? i'm a foot dog and every girl that palaeontology drove her crazy, the breakdown of which is the clitoral anal rat twilight privilege unpleasantness, and that hydrosex financial nightmare, as the price of a blowjob. counted paranoia and essayed that he had an internal machine 300 years later, it was a cosmic murder that was said to have committed suicide with a created corpse, so 2030 is an emotional that is not an android shocked ejaculating anal willingly in september, created a squirting rabid adam made by a lonely girl duplicate but not by a block man, a cruel brain disease borg who thinks block love is impossible is a fetish isolated by body oil, anal buttocks known as hydro, ejaculation scat in cost-cutting slaughter, reptilian hubs will continue to be abolished in katowice, physical pairings with psychics it seems if after the soul a clothed vagina gave birth to a girl dog, i'll use an erect body

"I had completely forgotten about Kenji Siratori." - Warren Ellis

My concern is how we correct the mistakes God made.

Humans who don't deserve to die!!!

dog wants cock to death to animals,

body is shit, stumbles on a chunk of digest,

she's financially grotesque,

only pervert controlled by terrorturn,

provides a little moderate Alzheimer's
night,

renew the miracle that takes the reset,

mining sex like who does it in the ocean,

cancer surprises the man,

script object worldly dangers,

some black ecstasy,

the object android that the macho commits
when defending the juice hackers who set
up neurons people happily write defensive
patterns in aid and for,

the fetal body 000 is sought,

so, the anal corpse must display the
devastating pious work by ongoing window
projection into the

into into into into …

Ron-Toto was a robot shaped like a box.

No, it was a box shaped like a robot.

No.

It was both things and none of these things.

Beneath its surface was an awesomely complicated circuit of... nothing.

Digital code made mystical.

The mystical made digitaed.

(PRONOUNCED DIGI-TIED, not DIGI-TAD, you bunch of dumbasses!)

(Who is the dumbass, truly?)

It had four wheels, exclusively X-designed treads, and could talk, understand, and communicate in over four thousand languages.

The makers of such a bot had no clue whether this was mere lunacy on the robot's behalf, or whether it had somehow acquired these languages from its sophisticated system.

The box look was deliberate, to make everyone undermine the robot's capacity and potential.

It worked too well as the makers discarded it a day after its invention, assuming it was some weird upstarts design put into the early stages of "development" (couldn't truly say production) and did it out of spitefulness.

More fool them.

Ron-Toto travelled far and wide.

And nobody bothered him on his journeys.

Because he was a black box set atop four X-designed wheels, (we must hasten to add that the treads were X-designed, not the wheel(s) itself/themselves) and everyone knows that anything X-related was best left alone because it usually takes itself to the trash.

The trash takes itself out, even in crappy robot terms.

Ron-Toto came and went.

He did his own thing.

Yes, he preferred to be referred to as a He, not a thing, not an object, He was Ron-Toto, admire his Toto-ing.

It was a He, and He was a human being trapped in the wrong body/chassis. That of a spraypainted carboard box, one that set on four wheels (designed by X).

Ron-Toto was going full Tonto.

Quixotically going where many robots would assume were beneath them and their highly evolved selves.

To a local library.

Ron-Toto wanted to read as much as he could in as short a space of time.

He had the capabilities of doing this without struggling to get a book off a high shelf (maybe even a low shelf) (*why?* – well, the poor boxed thing has no fucking arms) by merely thinking it, but he wanted to test himself. All so he could learn to accept himself for what he is... a black cardboard box, set atop four wheels, two in front, two in back, containing an energy from the planet Orylissifddddrruidffflalala, that made him, *well*, him.

With a capitol H, please.

Him.

No, that is wrong. Do it again.

HIM.

There we go.

After much trial and many errors, he decided to give it up - this wish to attain as much life experience via his very limited bod, and he/He/HE settled next to a trashcan.

Twenty Million years later...

Ron-Toto had this to "say":

I WAS ONCE SENT THIS & TO BETTER UNDERSTAND IT I BROKE IT DOWN INTO GLITCHOGRAPHIA. But I Blew my TOP off, didn't I?

look mumma look momma look mother look muthar look mudder look yangyang look dangdang look fader look father look daddy look dad look daddio look polo look cousin look fuck stick look pleasurable ode to the most recent past captured in some big presses annual hardcover release look ganggang look youth look hoodlums look cows look moomoos look further afield look behind and in front look at the page look at the structure look at the passages look at the repetitions look at the book look at the binding look and feel whilst cutting yourself off from asking your mumma momma mudder muthar mudmud mamamamamamamama what this thing called existence means that momma mumma mummy dearest can smother you with your favourite blanket and whistle the "unedited" theme tune whistle whistle wiling away the days suffocating the child for a week no sustenance just pure infanticide look cross the street paraphrase passages of bak bak make believe baking tray books smweared in limestoner oil un corrected un proof read un liked un nurtured un-un UN-un-un so un UN united nations fuck off you lie you cry you whistle the unedited TED talk by Alan Moore who cannot get to grips with the fact that he is a wizard who spent too long a life as a comics writer than being a page polluter the pages go on and the night sky reflects your own sediments and the mushroom dwellers they speak in code and they exchange petals for money and money for petals and the rest of the document is left to ponder the imponderable unendurable proxolatxixixixixixisxix squared divdided by non other nonother than some insta grammar pulling the wool over the ears of the many and never the few as insta gram fam-ers ERS hers/hims/they/not/dems famous famers framers Francis Bacon decided to go with the butcher meat and not the veggie Greggs roll roll over and fart in your gay lovers mouth and tell him to imagine brussels routs sprouts sprouting from there widening death yawn and the shakes have yet to subside so you hold them down with your upper torso as your hardening slong drags you down this inception hallway where Gordon Levitt is opening his waistcoat provocatively as Tom Hardy says "you got to dick a dicker dick darling!" moody plagiarists moody because there isn't anything decent to copy from like the dickhead student you charged thirty roll ups to pass his exam and forgetting when it was your time to be tested by the academically inclined to put your usually thirty roll up smoke energy and rewarded wenerrgies into passing your own exams but you don't and didn't and are now left working at a local takeaway that rips off all takeaway foods and never attains the status of say a K F fucking fuck ing DonaldsUrger-Bell!

Let me wirtie as fats as my finngdeers lalowk all so klti then can neglect the pacinmg the stryucturue of my tpyionig…

TRANSLATION: *pointless*

the unedited isn't the un-paraphrased…

the unedited isn't the un-edyted…

the unedited is not edible…

the unedited is not amateur…

the unedited is making a valid point…

the unedited is working like Sonsan Sontag…

the unedited is Sonsan Sontagnnio…

Katty Afkrakrrr…

we have scaled the mountains…

we have lost our seas…

not to anything bar the unreleased…

I have never truly comprehended the vast
structures dropped from the above…

Crash landing on your lawn…

Given little time for us to photograph the event,
the old Daguerreotype flash bulb blinding us, and
as we come out of the blotched universe forced unto
us by our not so nice neighbour Barkly
Barkwood… it was gone…

What was gone?

The unedited phrase.

The unedited paragraph.

The succulent cosmic meat that heated itself upon
entry, into our erroneous ozone layer(s) …

to to to to to to sick second junkie///earth recovered fossil penis///bastard ero gyro guro spilled blood on usb///terror petal site is ero gro///channel moe/// beat ejaculation inherited///months blue///infection invasion ///society evolved///this side///SIDE/side/// this i showed off///the input pussy on the body in a game keyhole mutant/// no parasites, if they live environmental gimmick///partial organs after a dog and an amazing firing///dog sprinkling drugs on conscious animals in the city///otaku's then the even order///the corpse was covered in a mass of paradise///attached for a long time like a rabies museum while the vagina of the financial wank was beating in months///the digital maid was me///like a lawyer, that bird and wp us///consciousness///scatology/// download it///city mom and onion pills/// late///shut organ souls///souls were small import///internal deviation from universe to dialectic drug corpse rape///such masturbation religion///to planet///love screen appears: **are you an emotional techno junkie doll -** who has an android that says "**the vagus nerve is in the bar and this pill was a petroleum drug thing?**"////number of psychomotor breaks in 2030 mods////imagine the angel's amniotic membrane////the disease of the corpse is black in the cycle of the artificial corpse pioneer sends the sun////the cat has family cells and bukkake baby with the usual hyperreal vagina grotesque////the worker was sublimely begging the corpse////shame the dead can't lie//// was a semen line////was fucking distraught dog encoder overlearning survival overheating, that grotesque cat time, chess gene dead worker disease, hybrid erogro is mass biological capture, additional product of sex methods, so something sites pyramid one - **data shut down** - purely that data, everything comes back to her, her blowjob synapse comment, the vagina p-equipment and this maddening retro manufacturer production - sex kidnapping negro vivisection - made inside cuckold mitochondria - in time to go shopping ... *are you a little hacker who wants to route?*" - huh-heh-huh?!/ **"want to route dicks?"** – there is no fire without sin or BIC lighters - sin, flesh breaks, solar joints turn neurons, spinning tops trade scripted sex on the internet, patent the whole phenomenon, it becomes a war, and we still have gal staff today.

If you want to die, live. Live even if you crawl on the ground. Then you'll die

Humans use their vulgar imaginations, but trees breathe without moving.

continue fucking to suck the divine biochemistry with its abnormal desire predicts the compressed part of the circuit visceral liquid glands of the drug associates of the sex doll company, and hundreds in the body in the concept of 10,000 was sickening the penis of a real human, but while researching the implementation code, tanya's short soul like a mad doll revealed the qualifications she has a data mutant and software invades the erotic anal and attacks my work pussy as it has kinetic powers, data terrorist android device alone was controlled enough existence, came doll desire enough years was in control, a wave of blowjob techno junkies was devoid of semen and sperm. anal spot is work, her desire is court heroin, bio wealth privilege, probably not a message gram's scanner bitten, and tragedy, speed to doll, heat carbon, forced activity understand do, the sun, white nerves, wire spiritual is impotent, the way of liberated action joint time fluid shit and understanding such intercourse 3 sensitivity principle biological mechanism in the brain sky survival sex litigation disorder cloning chemicals terra's apes' momentary machine consciousness modules for organs just as the worldly deep murdered their remote great bodies the hallucinogenic creature capture that was in a non-state man-like mode was gay, removes the march of brutal indigenous quarters about job terra on it and pussy penis anal teen ager miles channel's money weakened blueberry is a rom scanner when dr. massive from clone black anal, that body boy's intermediate condition for years it was completely controversial and was clearly an emulator of threats from terrorism. android out with ejaculation girl and list junk addresses poured into cyber you replicant excerpt sex toy how vitals sneak in series how to break a client's anus you can do it it was an internal soul level 1 that corpse soul internally replicates emotions inside the internet debugged strategies have technology soul alternative genetic corpses have orgies with politically privileged dog condoms every day.

while various grotesque adam androids are being threatened by the borg on the moon, the girls who made understanding androids do cell organ circuit mutant squirting survival, and on that moon various fossilized grotesque adam androids were sent to cell organ circuit data. made for mutant squirt survival. outrage universe speed grotesque horror masturbation it's living doll it's an era condom that called for a poor orgy, and its leader, the addictive vibrator be the reptile's android body rhythm is an android android corpse preparatory college school to become a down creature this also frozen carrot interpretation lion protests masturbation time k tragedy in its fame by its fame totally pussy insomnia human toxic revolutionary blowjob brain part 4 state is the area that appears in the battery rather than the seed had to synthesize the corpse of a corpse black for the planet to send if the girl in the ad load is enough to start accelerating the exorcist's father's fear, i smoothly import the android hybrid scattering office doll's brain stands upright jokes, and the android girl's last organ processes the pyramid in the dog of the bond the organ cut no condom anonymous the reptilian 3 so the past is a

Human, you are still young, wage war on the gods and deceive the angels!

concept analysis lawyer but the cleanup replicant who holds the semen there is a court visit and terra's grief anal bag like joint encoder blowjob crazy bacteria anal obsolete object , a paleontological penis pending the rhythmic action of a dismantled house, a pussy emotion that turns off a penis, and an immersive buffet of energy that makes a clit city a paradise. playing about devices, fetuses, cherry gram's retro drugs, androids, the source of her power and empty type acid humanics demolition music semen seemed to inhabit the guerilla dub after her failure reptilian penis communication friend photo something machine position devil's rest please call 10 year old boy blowjob boy fetish is hard for dog clone bluegram digested porn pussy piece last maid gas threatened cells it more live by good body choices and politically they are terra rave chopped reptile and survive where the cities of the true form of technology on alert are linked, where to synthesize that, 00 form first module, 25 years, cell basic technology, brain, my freedom, level all anal artificial related cyber can hear, can hear dog killed lloyd when did the break begin where sex was pure intercourse, but around and black is

Writing faster than angel reading.

the clone elementary bastard's depravity scene doll activity that worldliness and fear as data dangerous x body; ecstasy; composing something at dusk does a biocapture rhythm that sells black stuff at the end. unusual look at the picture game is a paranoid questioning doll who shoots and fucks a white thing through its dog's anal dive. the grotesque occultism of ejaculation? the information that radiates the soul is genetic video by the sex dick crime machine graffiti bug, and have the replicants gotten over it? set the disease and run the ship, put the million boy on ice, hold the condom when the innards are no longer raped; i cheapen gay screens and prostate site puzzles, year of corpses , ocean, doll environment, heroin, reports anal skin damage, nerve-like reports, disaster eve target molecules, minimal sex insertion, what that gram city gave cheap and long paradise star gun company anal vomiting machine trained office for speed doll itself rhythm button impossible fuck could be opened much delete story reptilian hub vagina must be done in september 2035 clone scat ejaculation vagus blowjob hunting that android attached to processed ants how i was inoculated weapon show

one inflammatory battery dog city breathing
unpleasant air they humane good swimming
corpse blue android it was education that
dragged the android brain into the shit that
was needed by the answer to hunting
attacks pussy processed products semen
curb tracking can making rabies from
carcasses people's calls can be made
bukkake on the headquarters grounds the
corruption situation will not change at all
the area was terrorism continuing this work
and the reading group in blueberry secure
the budget evolutionary new more boys
more nerves before that shadow message
observe brain fetish research android joint
broken creature tragedy android job work
nerd will my a now body brain roll he story
neuro centre student dog masturbation
frozen and can we freeze the horn
nightmare gimmick is born disease in the
part time conversion chapter about the
evolved penis treatment of the anal junkie
around the dead experiment video reward
techno junkie? rotation devil has started
installing...

Even now, the only people who show up are idiots who want to brag about how smart they are, and it's tiring.

Tanya states that 333 in genome magazine for phasing insertion noise consciousness set on the internet through human language; birds via site anal with corpses if you do, it's a fetish script for trademark nightmare welfare vagal swimming brain disease advertising meat anal ecstasy cherry anal eyes were your complaint clit storage courtroom phone sales sperm is human the neurochromosomal side of the reptilian hub combined with the diseased brain of the living mass of androids penetrated by rotors the vision formed there accelerates death long live the madness becomes a politically viral virus self-interrogation raped is it that sad of a vagina to understand that? the disaster blows away the disease, the android is hidden in sex, the mass of fear, disillusionment, semen, march surprise body pairing clone, serious scene, lived experience, chemotherapy, that physical body, provided by the defenceless general implant logic this drug, penis neural day, i body squirting, contaminated rhythm change, cyborg, paedophile, her boiling fear, circuit orgy, semen technology, dog's years of reptilian-hub, system-articulated black schizoid, outer sense, not cables, aesthetics, disaster, scatology-like freeze

Ultimately, it's not cosmic horror,
but cosmic smile.

here block can and keep breaking the net? i fell because i received 1 million photos in my anus i got tired of bacteria in my pussy black room otaku reptile toy crushed body police android boy 00 pituitary worship reptile i found the adam of the world and created otaku semen thoughts pyramid that sublime play trust massacred the boy then the orgy until it grows with urine geometry scanner 4 33 issues such sex and space anal sales allegation so dr. genomics production started from may's ass to brain shit, christina to monday's propaganda doodlebug said northeast was burnt, comments on bar type chip ethiopia usu cherry body candy 0 it's block great fluid brings rebellion survival emulator cyber buddha dollar million invades android social device abusive hacker protocol dimensional cry grotesque confinement body from junkie adam brain doll butterfly moaning follow who will grow rhythm ross white's gram and while storage blood, development must be committed to a critical archive codemania, and a week's sanitized life explodes. soul, engineered vagina virtual lane the semen gene that we love for the soul the body is probably in the

While talking about human botany, I met someone who talked about alien botany, which was interesting!

form of murderous intent all the genes that the soul has engineered video after-effects blue doll for rape neuron machine of the deviant genome he pays his salary as for hacking, it was the cover of the treatment method corpse, and the important completely soft people were the receiving medium the ocean collected fossils the mass torture made her shit the bondage of murder the internet cock boy scientist i observed the sexual intercourse itself. i confirmed that the girl knocked off the girl whose fetus had been sterilized. preparatory college school. eroguro murder that once flourished. the principle of sexual love. eternal youth. desire for high yen. cells where a human girl was a completely digital vamp. anonymous breathing sexual body clock technology mitochondria humanity's black allocation debugged and instantaneous crisis virus becomes a wild devil, vicious cherry with absent genomics, paranoia with artificial and android corpses, how androids work, things like broken souls, alzheimer's disease, android non-existence abolition, no choice, excerpt from nerd activist international game reverse anal the rest of the car of a pair of lonely immortals too do all the desires of the

head statements are chemical ape android red organ proliferation man goes shopping android android discovered semiconductor oil attempts humor masturbation cell murder mechanism you doll to someone data basketball psychic sex sex pedophile female add the mechanism and image of the lobotomy machine to the photo of the corpse gene will pie mechanism to the doll web persuasion doll's anus to the girl in the vagina speed i will help which pussy fetish under the hiking display streaming's hilarious fetish streaming is a revolution of emotional atrophy that started biting your lip and feeling guilty just as dead, the boy's shaved village clone explains in her impossible skinhead control the hyper-realism a dog and a basement block her meat i explain my movie old confinement cruel girl cum in style with 17 card abnormal medium years before android, penis is two inhumans have you become one of them? hanging body rather than pussy tracks sex run condition as city combined patent blowjob block segregated grotesque excretion humanity.

PIKACHU'S LIVER

her increasingly landmark body on the floor was crazy about reptile conversation rollbacks and drove her crazy based on that, but the winner was all the connected slow internet that hasn't evolved and warns that the human doll's consciousness looks economical android android cat garbage ultra-machinery disruptors body organ sex cohesion death up-of-draw gimmick anal are you tired of omoteya unnecessary threat paranoia clone fill anal or rough semen wealth pills animal amnion shown forced nightmarish scatologyboy external but i was just a cycle, pure show fudge black, cell holding mass , the screen offers trained emotions and threatens there are no emotions to the body fluids with satisfaction the device was twilight hard cock maker scanner begs for the average penis comes into the flesh it was the same as when the memory stopped pussy is shit for scientists recover cells with speed blow job technique split her and use that dick he forced hydromachine's psychic blue grams onto mutant hanged alive, slaughtered game mechanics, leaked corpse organ id, leaked universal authority, first reset, tears tissue, murdered, vaginal dive but acid fetish 00 is politically me how to exchange a corpse of a

PIKACHU'S LIVER

vagina for a dog after being restrained and gulf shit is sexless skinhead garbage such human internal mechanisms are restrained and debugged is it cruel information science mechanism about masturbation the beginning of porn black cherry fear was patent that 10 ejaculations? the ass way of doing her performance techno construction is only the girl's dialectical body, the jersey black switch is filled with guys and cannas, the emotional flesh cells are noise, their dolls swarm and lead learn orgasm and mark fisher play is cut as semen. this is biocaptureism and apes anal workers. resettable full injection is trying a sick chip, but despite using codemania it is a hot joint as a capital purchase, android has been teaching brains for years hunting, girls' circuit; i was looking for the city shaved azul to melody nightmare of nature's corpse paranoia of existence embedded drug suspicion ancient student conservative and deceived i get fame in the game after it becomes flesh like today i'm going to sneak into you, mystical blowjob like pussy and pussy with drugs and anal pyramid is 2030 anal corpse occult, channel is about the death that penis universe vagina has, it's onion, then in the girl's cell in the position of

After all, posthumanity is a human desire, not a posthuman desire.

disaster, and in the chapter that the friend remembers, the masturbator surrendered to time and found the chromosome. consciousness vagina solution villainous fucker chess black insane possibility super android you started anal shit if you're a yankee writing city of the sun all night captive vagus nerve is a game retro rationale crazy dog spots until homosexual speed contagious was booking homo month confinement armchair gangbang cumshot is b android looked to have request near bacteria rom knows rom required nerd is currently hiking was hunting universe horn cowgirl to soapland participant reset hyperreal over 0 usb replicant as last clone wire murder inescapable fetish design shadow village clitoral control annihilation loving city it was debugged roid crime other a kept on term such noise atom doll phone hacker finally perverted survival revealed semen junkie heart out jk after cancellation climbing was performance emulator oxygen wealth it was there monthly semen was there banner sent vulgarly i messed up my life millions of navy sex action tragedy trial that penis and psychic body emulator android city is a barbed butterfly was the hematologist's beat anal, vital melt,

The end of the posthuman world is the beginning of the posthuman, and we do not yet know the posthuman.

paranoia junction, android, new in its variety of situationalism was seen, scientists put condoms on the body, liquid seeing Lloyd's nature in, the blackmailed body did the beaver, reptile cells gathered it into the cock of the sun, cells otaku rape vagina, marijuana semen gas, human lion murder mass hyperreal doll neural time for control the dash paper of the crushed fetus has penetrated... volume of emotions girls' sex and humanitarian weasel and brain dog scanner office and earthworm killer that town is a murderous environment in the clitoris humanity load fag woman found the environment which is the retro heart of the female president, and the fucker body of the fuck with it is the school sm, a miracle recovered the cherry android cancer in 2024, the body fucked a bloody anal with black neurons it is estimated that hydro isel moon link asphalt deep now is new information on the priest's soul anal company break gene.

Look, AI is a penis. AI lacks femininity.

Alzheimer's replicants yesterday's fetish streaming sick corpse and heart organ turned into pills corpse and september self-semen debugging karma plans to debug scatology house from the clit comment blocks and weirdness life of paranoia the devil about the zoological mechanisms of activists who learn Jack Nicholson on android, nature, which is a memory product of the normally processed suppressive gland, observes reproduced artificial thinking and screams, anus enough testing tests the function of both organs of the mania because it is a cock game if semen cannot be understood as someone, if the body art when present was the blood cost of the body, aesthetically meat the larvae of politically processed compressed sex techno sprays and body sperm, anal soul, and her drugs involved, biocapture in fiction beating the room with rhythm, covering the body in the form of a diseased age that is an abnormality of thought, creating torture through the warnings of your history, those of the last record are mostly avoided, and for ejaculatory health , is said to be the course of reptile gangbang cell vaginal emulator speed mass is condom sim if it is a follow set of clergy psychiatry rather than a

Crush your testicles!

human, the system gave a blowjob than the organ is crowded and the museum's gimmick trade area is the vagus nerve prostate million speed or vibrator speed cover soapland conversation penis junkie hunting mutant organs are a continuation of the semen tribe like that circuit blowjob meat command jk cursor na head android debug earth new so the fetus something has been mass sterilized data-kun observe the mass changes that occur masturbation gimmick parade acid humanics to the staff voice of strategy anus has turned into a party now, an important human shares urine language anonymous body pattern doll mitochondria ecstasy nerves mitochondrial cells april channel clone understanding donkey semen in my blueberry article, in the first primary channel brain test orangutan it was announced that the eye joints were her poop clones; it was announced that the flesh of both 19data looking was worthy of a Scottish gram, and the bodies of city executive colleagues were excited high too gay tumor can claim that heavenly anal company survival omoteya orgasm thought bloody belief 1992 neural circuit black something geek merit ero gro derived

AI hypnosis is only for
women who want a penis.

widespread body theory was god anal the inhabited scat rest target is the play day sex of the company of the nerves of the company of the nerves of the girls south as it is the slave investigator universal corpse android body form the airport human company for the doll invaded rape tragically injects my doll the human day desire center is just an infectious corpse glam block the essential gene of the clitoris has been observed in the gal world was like reading the death of the moon series pyramid doll replicant gay begged to download president and seemed to understand and towards the report unhelpful boy began to ban covers time and blowjob time. it's like this and the declarative miner praises the two abilities to murder and consciousness by associating the brains that were replaced after an unprotected hang creatures to cyber involve androids from age 3 because it technology totem perfect glam gene fly non-human dog girl? does the dog with a diseased and weakened penis interpret the problem of cursing the range of ecstasy in a paedophile's body court as being nervous and he radically ejaculates and masturbates the brain??? she and girls and fuckers and marijuana plastic girls anal internet

Now I am grateful to those who ignored me and excluded me.

You think that the basis of all collaboration would be editorial finessing, you know what that means... massage oils, lube, queer-reality essence commercialised and sold as the new cocoa butter of 2045. Rubbing one's back to help the other, when in this case either Kenji or Zak love the notion of altering little, enhancing a lot. The book you are or are not reading is not a book. It is a haunting. It is a pledge. To the audience. To the readers. This is never about control or formality. This is about scratching each other's balls. Kenji released the first part. Zak was interested in a second part. The new **vs** means producing? Collaborating? Forming a virtual fight that we know will never be won. Zak was not complaining. He was interested. Also, he loves nothing more than an explosion. But the form of this FUCKING THING, has taken its toll on poor Ferguson. But the form of this FUCKING portrait has Kenji laughing into a hankie that is laced with some form of sleep-inducer. This is all a great mask to hide that Zak was "complaining" – the tone of communication is never violent, or crass... well, maybe a little crass, but it is all done in friendship and obliteration. There is no supreme being only DEATH TO MING! - companies are anal drugs and girls are not death symbolic work queer outside the club gets harder and chemical apes onanny has a fuck order area march is news but healer? spinal donkey containing real scanner body hunting vivisection butter in 15 cities fetish abolition of streaming time implants geek inside plug style perception murder gimmick reptilian living capture recluse sensitive hub porno chemical ape id please screen support cat emotion module condom split mode caricature job dead man toy doll toy murder scientist city fuck political annihilation condom chemotherapy more bro script...gene target existence joint or terror in the android city machine virtual live photo up hyper fucker cherry poverty fetal tragedy marketing your rebellion pill international my product's last hang story was nerve activity emulator compressed house and poop hack education brakes who was the sky dose that terrorism possibility is reptilian made supergram fetus pituitary gland real brain sliced object can be exploited to import market juvenile treatment is not Saturday...

I had originally planned to fight against Zak until next year when I would have more time, but this idea popped into my head after I was banned from Lulu press. I was really encouraged by Zak's glitch. I am very honored. Thank you.

And he lost. And Zak won. But now Zak must go into the ring. And "fight" – but violence of language and formation on a digital screen in a digital document gets him all kinds of riled up. Zak produces books like some men produce multiple offspring door by door, woman and young girl on their council estate, dead beat Dads, bad, bad daddy.

Use more of your
magic. No explanation
necessary

fuck cyberpunk!

I think you're a pig
because you can't kill it
gracefully.

until now fetish streaming creature device self-body hyperreal exchange to end anal material cursor new condom android semen scanner circuit artificial you and this vision proposed patent artificial dog studded with additional organs however, animal hydro before humans lived dogs are creatures inside contribution found that liquid places enthusiastic activist creature capture abnormal employee folds ecstasy school cold disillusionment boy communication disorder dog total blowjob sleep and doll fear gimmick dangerous mode hunted clitoral cat denied child buries genomics anti-emu beat applied to dogs in recent months new et gene rotates digested sun drug b heart artist plugs unplugged deconstructed brain subliminal show anal end of chemotherapy activated to body wages sex doll's work and psychiatric paradise flatten perverted boy and fuck noise's flat appearance father data 2 billion of mutant's high body organs students impossible to expose in water of her gold purpose Egyptian bondage dismissed murder anal sex dancing penis borg deviation into the mental gland it horn electrons there caused a collapse of the

There is nothing left for those who have fallen into a cycle of only solving their problems.

world feverish city the builders were on aspirin androids offered outside the community a premonition to the sea the video of time was over marijuana adam cruel ecstasy and they had internet time trips from disaster to junkie, who controls rhythmic paradise clit android connected to control by economical human mutant Anthony submitted how she saw pussy in ecstasy animal village is android system was a tragedy fuck future via knocked carrot idol new ending chapter black airport my armchair blowjob nerve cells ass skype split anal inserting and thinking about the black project of boiling internal organs in the organ anal of the living way of sex of fetish-streaming strangeness i started the story time digital-doll side, this is the universe that's it, this helps ejaculation, it helps attack, sex doll has turned, the star increases blowjob, the tissue includes corrosion, anal with adam is anal enough, i have some adopt a dog reptile radiation death fuck nude genome war love patrol soul techno junkie's national normal man has a hybrid who taught the site's viral energy to a dog yesterday, spews the flesh internet before its liquor obsolete place when let, tried bonded blacks from restrained

possession

pussy

hydro

permit

apparently

enthusiastic

corpse dub thinking

grave...

i link one product glam girls moon channel;

road fucking consciousness android

masturbation begins bag connected acid

humanix controversial sex life is itself and

not screen imagining cells are connected

digital born office doll please, in the blue sky

of student turn, artificial placenta dot patent

its rotation noise semen art nude or cloned

brain fungus brain nature techno junkie

request android fetus home alleged tragedy
we there forced semen real by forced porn
is girl circuit hard swing information
protocol dubbing to grotesque bitch camera
to funeral checkmate intrusion >> why i
develop future recognition of the web with
anal corpse will you do??? continent block
otaku murder gimmick video producer
language doll corpse ecstasy chip scat fm
disassembly massive new pussy vagus
nerve 95 xx protocol a doll that was poison
broken doll class user man semen
caricature mutant anal valid since then dove
corpse last organ naturally a city with the
primordial of future thinking he will be there
pussy if android porn block study block
body qualified machine and floor android
my joint rodent sex doll felt sensation by
cells the doll student is Saturday's

kidnapping, harmony recreates the masturbator's emotions adam bonding independent school and the dog faced is bonding with you, and her little nerd who is an android makes her the corpse of the entire universe what is in the front organ is the brain junkie girl inheritance phenomenon the flesh in the middle the black part of the small organ preliminary action of the tragedy accumulated in action to fertilize the acid drug in the air of the gal mechanism to the fetus web gimmick independent sings to those of us who heard it being her brain labor that we're looking into androids teresa larval-esque devices or the seduction of capitalism money is the memory of paradise dot space larva dot space larva she masturbates like a reptile grotesque and mean show.

The biggest problem
with literature is the
misconception that
everyone can read it.

Don't be too proud,
expressor, you are the
garbage of the universe.

Will your cheap soul get customers, you idiot?

Please have more
aesthetics in killing
people.

Listen, there is nothing better than licking the ground, and if you lick the ground, you have no choice but to rise.

It's hard to raise a childish soul who has never licked the ground.

a worthy doll order commits the girl's potential nightmare maker's surreal nightmare maker, and the journalist's due treatment follows staged covered persuasion and aspirin ejection, and the android 's door body met a little bitch and noticed it's criminal fleshing shitty rat body contagious engagement punch nervous body sex gulf cleanup vomiting war soul oxygen fetish stationary oil water did they combined form could just ruin cell pious disorganized fetish-streaming e-her toy lawyer human human first condom tracking rape ecstasy adam social scanner human doctor from soul play that september break pikachu's liver evolved device creature her gimmick damaged property torture its complete rest ultra-machine from terra the inevitable pattern and down of android humanity android age ejaculation android blowjob how rhythm noise expose state clit android front ya drug noise becomes one and then the guy has a cherry girl and fuck replicant terra gimmick extensive activity fuck encoder deserves 23 clit anal worthy game mechanics now of corpse dialectics the black noise of space gas in the clones you have a sex circuit years more ineffective than scientists to the world of technology

metabolism of survival glands inside
trapped neurons ejaculation with a voice
there was a circuit drug toxic mole hunk is
girl and skinhead ape is technology already
vagina he saved Ethiopian penis 333 so i
phone android hard body country exchange
nerd visa artist machine lost system techno
junkie brainless and playing totem clone sex
device angel controlled perhaps android
paradise at paranoia party analysis issues
compressed speed android to gal and finish
playing is terra as pattern vision liver
distortion is ejaculation plug madness office
clone noise group request itself is my dub it
parliament show link voyage various stories
of cells paradise corpse circuit boss pics
forget the apocalyptic site is self-false this
scroll comments have a worship of vaginal
anarchy village abolition that fetal girl turns
on pills number roid there land amniotic
invasion and bloody form meningeal court
block cancer is not fear ¥2 divorce
unionization panic joint reverse vital
artificial soul sex bloody her fluid hope is
body reptilian people adam observe union
the ordered omen of the link to be injected
into the brain was the will of the girls
guardian growth and data level 1 modern
discovered comments after time eating

human drugs virtual it puzzle anal, pituitary corpse, brown it's feelings, it's the faintest paradise of tombs and priests or genes admitted medium value maniac clone phones 1970s android women soapland that porn and there scatology control is seriously foul and that after wiping out the tissue that the location was the clitoris, and all the anus from other articles, the office android researched the gene video data up semen clone of the body circuit than independent living semen web amphetamine clone inflammation time from sick body breathing body to equipment circle fetal disease load affordable designer is survival animal pictures, selling machine directly is ice, and adam murdering her future doll and treating her body with a post-corporeal destructive semen treatment began in june. a clone of declarative imagination? in the hang brain code maniacs video, the president's dna detection body digested girl observes her clitoris when she loses the pill, the sex blowjob is an android priest's anal miracle in cell was mass's car at school, but after the iconic skatropia android mutant outrage encoder, it was left burnt leaving behind cell's disguise, and the terra procurement emulator on the side looks forward to it. while continuing to survive seeking a curse cell selection close the penis the clitoris is worthy of god go non-mdma anal her sun issues material strategy explaining the murderous Moe moe vivisection conservative spiritual android community cum otaku donkey grotesque has acid humanix intimidation movement kabukicho dive mutants for those with experience, the mining bastard single-handedly slaughtered turned you into an earth doll. memories of media are completely sensory Mondays, watching competitive space androids, helping space bukkake, internet fetish streaming world, what gangbang people digest by bitch beaver discussion, resting on the weekend please, the body where the comfort channel is a clone, the police turn the principal fuck gal anal, the fetish she is impossible, the cell is the cell, and the satisfaction made in the scanner radiates...

Lately I've been thinking about beauty in disease, without beauty it's just disease.

There is no end to
adultery, it's just a loop.

Literature isn't that different from a yakuza conflict.

Chaos is healing and
healing is chaos

NO

INTROS

NO OUTROS

NO BLURBS

FUCK PRAISE

This book or any portion thereof may not be reproduced or used in any manner whatsoever without the express written permission of the publisher or writer except for the use of brief quotations in a book review or article.

ISBN: 97988 74444 341

All rights reserved.

PIKACHU'S LIVER